EMMA
Every Day

Cat Care

by C.L. Reid

illustrated by Elena Aiello

PICTURE WINDOW BOOKS
a capstone imprint

Published by Picture Window Books, a Capstone imprint
1710 Roe Crest Drive
North Mankato, Minnesota 56003
capstonepub.com

Library of Congress Cataloging-in-Publication Data
Names: Reid, C. L., author. | Aiello, Elena (Illustrator), illustrator.
Reid, C. L. Emma every day.
Title: Cat care / by C.L. Reid ; illustrated by Elena Aiello.
Description: North Mankato, Minnesota : Picture Window Books, [2024]
Series: Emma every day | Audience: Ages 5 to 7. | Audience: Grades K-1.
Summary: Emma is eager to foster Mittens the cat, but she did not anticipate the chaos a cat can cause--but than Mittens disappears.
Identifiers: LCCN 2022044500 (print) | LCCN 2022044501 (ebook)
ISBN 9781484675656 (hardcover) | ISBN 9781484675670 (paperback)
ISBN 9781484675663 (pdf) | ISBN 9781484675717 (kindle edition)
ISBN 9781484675724 (epub)
Subjects: LCSH: Deaf children--Juvenile fiction. | Cats--Juvenile fiction.
CYAC: Deaf--Fiction. | People with disabilities--Fiction. | Cats--Fiction.
Classification: LCC PZ7.1.R4544 Cat 2024 (print) | LCC PZ7.1.R4544
(ebook) | DDC [E]--dc23
LC record available at https://lccn.loc.gov/2022044500
LC ebook record available at https://lccn.loc.gov/2022044501

Summary: Emma fosters a cat named Mittens.

Image Credits: Capstone: Daniel Griffo, 28 (bottom),
Margeaux Lucas, 29 (bottom), Randy Chewning, 28 (top), 29 (top)

Design Elements: Shutterstock: achii, Mari C, Mika Besfamilnaya

Special thanks to Evelyn Keolian for her consulting work.

Editor's note: Throughout the book, a few words are called out and fingerspelled using ASL. Some of these words do have signs as well.

Designer: Bobbie Nuytten

Printed and bound in the USA. PO#5425

TABLE OF CONTENTS

MEET EMMA

EMMA CARTER
Age: 8 Grade: 3

SIBLING
One brother, Jaden
(12 years old)

PARENTS
David and Lucy

BEST FRIEND
Izzie Jackson

PET
a goldfish named Ruby

favorite color: teal
favorite food: tacos
favorite school subject: writing
favorite sport: swimming
hobbies: reading, writing, biking, swimming

FINGERSPELLING GUIDE

MANUAL ALPHABET

Aa   Bb   Cc   Dd   Ee

Ff   Gg   Hh   Ii   Jj

MANUAL NUMBERS

0   1   2   3

Emma is Deaf. She uses American Sign Language (ASL) to communicate with her family. She also uses a Cochlear Implant (CI) to help her hear.

Kk Ll Mm Nn Oo

Pp Qq Rr Ss Tt Uu

Vv Ww Xx Yy Zz

4 5 6 7 8 9 10

Chapter 1

Waiting and Waiting

Emma loved her pet goldfish,

Ruby. But Ruby just swam

in circles.

"Can we foster a cat?" Emma

signed.

"Sure," Emma's dad signed. "I will

call Cat Connections and sign up."

"Let's get ready while we wait," Emma signed.

"Good idea," Dad signed.

They went to the store. They bought a litter box,  litter, cat food, and cat dishes. Emma bought a toy mouse too.

Dad helped Emma set up the litter box in the bathroom. Emma put the cat dishes in the kitchen.

"Did they call?" Emma asked every day.

"Not yet," Dad said every day.

At last, Cat Connections called.

"They have a cat for you," Dad signed.

"Remember, you can only keep the cat for eight weeks," Mom signed.

"I know," Emma signed.

"That will still be fun," Jaden signed.

Chapter 2

Meet Mittens

The next morning, Emma put on her Cochlear Implant (CI).

"I will bring home a new friend today," she said to Ruby.

Ruby swam in circles in reply.

Emma's dad was waiting for her.

He was holding a pet

carrier.

At the animal shelter, a nice

woman put a cat in Emma's arms.

Emma petted the cat. The cat curled

up in Emma's lap

and purred.

"This is Mittens," the woman said.

"I will take good care of her," Emma said.

"We will call you when we have a home ready for Mittens," the woman said. "Thank you for taking care of her."

Emma carefully put Mittens in the carrier. Then she carried Mittens into the car. Emma sat next to the cat carrier.

When they got home, Emma carefully carried Mittens into her room.

"There, there, sweet Mittens," Emma said, holding onto the toy mouse.

But Mittens wasn't shy. She jumped onto Emma's bed. She curled up on a pillow.

"It looks like she likes her new home," Dad said.

Later that day, Emma walked into her bedroom. Crayons were scattered on the floor.

"Who made this mess?"  Emma signed.

"Mittens," Jaden signed.

Emma went into the bathroom.

Toilet paper was everywhere!

"Who made this mess?" she signed.

"Mittens," Jaden signed.

When Emma walked into the living room, she saw dirt  from a plant all over the floor.

"Let me guess. Mittens?" Emma signed.

"Yep. Making a mess is her idea of fun," Jaden signed.

Emma went to her room to get Mittens. But she couldn't find her anywhere! Mittens was missing!

Chapter 3
Missing Mittens

Emma's family looked for Mittens.

Mom looked in the closets and

cabinets. Jaden looked under the

furniture.

"I know we will find her,"

Jaden signed.

Dad looked in the garage.

"Maybe she will find you,"

he signed.

That night when Emma got ready for bed, she wished Mittens would sleep next to her. But Mittens was missing.

"Where is Mittens, Ruby?" Emma asked.

Ruby made more

bubbles

and kept swimming.

Emma took off

her CI and went

to bed. She did not

sleep well.

The next morning when Emma
woke, she looked across her room.

There sat Mittens, right next

to the fishbowl. She was watching

Ruby swim.

Emma laughed and petted the cat.

"You are Ruby's Mittens," she said.

Mittens waved her tail as Ruby

swam.

LEARN TO SIGN

cat

Pretend to pull whiskers
on face.

fish

Hold hand sideways
and wiggle.

happy

Make two small circles
at chest.

sad

Move hands down
in front of face.

home

Move hand up to cheek.

telephone

Bring hand to cheek.

morning

Move hand up and toward body.

night

Move hand down and away from body.

GLOSSARY

Cochlear Implant (CI)—a device that helps someone who is Deaf to hear; it is worn on the head just above the ear

deaf—being unable to hear

fingerspell—to make letters with your hands to spell out words; often used for names of people and places

foster—to provide temporary care to shelter animals

pet carrier—small boxes, crates, or cages used to move pets from place to place

shelter—a place where stray, lost, or abandoned animals live

sign language—a language in which hand gestures, along with facial expressions and body movements, are used to communicate

TALK ABOUT IT

1. Emma had to wait a long time for her foster cat. Talk about a time when you had to wait for something. Was the wait worth it?

2. Do you think fostering a pet would be easy or hard? Why?

3. How do you think Emma felt while waiting for Mittens?

WRITE ABOUT IT

1. Write about your favorite animal. Would it make a good pet or not?

2. Emma was worried she lost Mittens. Write about a time you lost something.

3. Write a paragraph about where Mittens goes after he leaves Emma's house. What kind of family adopted her?

ABOUT THE AUTHOR

Deaf-blind since childhood, C.L. Reid received a Cochlear Implant (CI) as an adult to help her hear, and she uses American Sign Language (ASL) to communicate. She and her husband have three sons. Their middle son is also deaf-blind. Reid earned a master's degree in writing for children and young adults at Hamline University in St. Paul, Minnesota. Reid lives in Minnesota with her husband, two of their sons, and their cats.

ABOUT THE ILLUSTRATOR

Elena Aiello is an illustrator and character designer. After graduating as a marketing specialist, she decided to study art direction and CGI. Doing so, she discovered a passion for illustration and conceptual art. She works as a freelancer for various magazines and publishers. Aiello loves video games and sushi and lives with her husband and her little pug, Gordon, in Milan, Italy.